BANZO'S SWORD

Kevin L. Michel

FROM KEVIN L. MICHEL

Acta Non Verba: Deeds, not words

Moving Through Parallel Worlds To Achieve Your Dreams: The Epic Guide To Unlimited Power

Steam Over Cold Steel

The Liberated Mind: Reclaiming Attention and Inner Authority

The Four Upgrades: Reprogram Your Mind, Mood, Memory, and Meaning

The Art of Inner Warfare: Tactics for the Battle Within

Mental Toughness: Strengthen Your Mind to Achieve Your Dreams

The Art of Peace

The 7 Laws of Quantum Power

HISTORICAL NOTE

Banzo's Sword traces its lineage to the oral teaching tales of the Yagyū family, sword instructors to the Tokugawa shoguns in the early Edo period (1600s). The clan's founder, Yagyū Muneyoshi, and his son Yagyū Munenori (1571 – 1646) refined Yagyū Shinkage-ryū, a style whose lessons on patience and ever-present awareness (*zanshin*) circulated from dojo to dojo. This work offers an original retelling while honoring those Edo-era roots.

CONTENTS

PROLOGUE –
BLADE IN THE RAIN

The fiercest storm tests the strength of the tallest cedar; in rain, even steel must learn to endure.

Night fell with a drowning hush over the Yagyu estate. The rain had begun as a whisper at dusk, but by the hour of the dog it was a relentless cascade. Water drummed on the roof tiles and overflowed from the eaves, turning the courtyard's sand garden into a muddied field of puddles. Under the flickering light of a lone lantern, two figures faced each other in the open yard – one blade drawn, one spirit trembling, as sheets of cold rain battered their shoulders.

Matajuro's heart pounded against his ribs, each breath sharp in his throat. His fingers were clenched around the hilt of his katana, damp with rain and sweat. Across from him stood his father, Lord Yagyu, as still as a granite statue in a storm, the older man's sword unsheathed and held low at his side. Lantern light and lightning flashes danced along the razor edge of his father's steel. The air between them was tight, humming with the unsaid challenge.

For years Matajuro had trained under his father's tutelage in this very courtyard, longing to one day be the inheritor of the Yagyu style. Ambition burned within him like a small, stubborn flame refusing to be extinguished by the downpour. He would prove himself worthy tonight. The young man swallowed rainwater and fear as he bowed, signaling readiness. His father returned the bow – a shallow nod, eyes never leaving Matajuro's stance.

A crack of lightning split the sky, and in the stark white flash, Matajuro lunged. His sandals splashed through puddles as he struck, steel singing through the rain. He aimed a diagonal cut at his father's shoulder – a committed strike, fueled by all the determination in his twenty years. For an instant, the blade held an image of victory in Matajuro's mind.

But Lord Yagyu glided backward with uncanny

ease. Matajuro's katana sliced only water and empty night. The older swordsman's counter came swift as wind. Matajuro sensed rather than saw the movement – a sudden presence at his flank. He wheeled, bringing his sword up just in time to parry a blow that fell like thunder. Steel met steel in a burst of sparks. The shock reverberated down Matajuro's arms, nearly numbing his grip.

He gritted his teeth and pressed forward, launching a flurry of strikes despite the ache in his arms. Rain blurred his vision; he fought by instinct and the faint outline of his father's form in the darkness. The yard echoed with the clash of metal and the patter of rain, an erratic rhythm of desperation. Matajuro's braid of black hair came loose, water streaming down his face, but he did not falter. Each strike was met by emptiness or the precise deflection of his father's blade. Each desperate swing left him more off-balance.

Lord Yagyu hardly seemed to move, yet he was always a fraction beyond reach. The older man's face remained calm, even sorrowful, as he watched his son exhaust himself. There was no anger in the master's eyes—only a steeled patience.

Matajuro attacked again, a diagonal slash arcing upward. In that heartbeat, a bolt of lightning illuminated the scene: father and son, swords crossing, rain frozen in white light around them. Matajuro saw his own reflection in his father's blade, eyes wide with exertion. In the next blink of darkness, his father vanished from in front of him. With a gasp, Matajuro whirled—too slow. Something cold and unyielding kissed the nape of his neck. He went rigid.

His father's katana rested just above the collar of Matajuro's kimono, its edge glinting dangerously close to flesh. Matajuro's own sword hung limp in his hand, its tip now pointed to the ground. The fight was over. Defeat crashed over him heavier than the rainfall.

For a long moment, there was only the sound of the rain, and Matajuro's ragged breaths clouding in the chill autumn air. Lord Yagyu withdrew his blade and stepped back. The older man's voice came soft, nearly drowned by the downpour, but each word struck Matajuro harder than any sword-cut:

"You are slow. Unfocused." His father's tone was measured, betraying no fury—only disappointment deep as the night. "I have taught you since you could hold a wooden sparring sword, and still your swordsmanship is mediocre."

Matajuro opened his mouth to protest, to plead

that he only needed more time, but the weight of shame held his tongue. Rainwater streamed down his face, indistinguishable from the hot tears threatening his eyes. He bowed his head, trembling, waiting for his father's next words as a prisoner awaits sentencing.

Lord Yagyu exhaled a long breath. Through the veil of rain, Matajuro saw his father lift his gaze to the dark sky. Finally, the old swordsman spoke, each syllable sharp and clear despite the downpour:

"I can do no more for you."

The lantern's flame sputtered behind its screen, casting erratic shadows. Matajuro felt his stomach clench. He looked up, meeting his father's eyes—hard eyes, forged in decades of battle and discipline. In them, Matajuro saw a verdict.

"You will not inherit my sword," his father said quietly. The finality in his voice cut deeper than any blade. "Tomorrow, you will depart from this house."

A thunderclap rolled overhead as if the heavens themselves rumbled at these words. Matajuro's legs nearly buckled. He caught his breath, the shock as cold as the rain soaking through his training robe. Disowned. Cast out. The realization struck him with a force of its own. This courtyard had been his entire world; the name Yagyu, his birthright and pride. Now he was to leave it behind.

He wanted to cry out, to beg for another chance, but under his father's stern gaze he knew it was useless. The decision had been made. In that moment, Matajuro felt as though the flame of his ambition were being doused, leaving only smoke and sodden ashes inside his chest. The rain kept falling, relentless and uncaring.

Lord Yagyu sheathed his blade with a hiss of steel on wood. He turned and walked towards the silhouette of the manor house, leaving Matajuro standing alone in the storm. Over his shoulder, the father delivered one final, quiet injunction: "If you truly wish to master the sword... seek Banzo."

Matajuro's breath caught. Banzo. He had heard the name whispered in respectful tones among his father's peers. Banzo was a legendary swordsman who had retired to seclusion in the mountains, a man said to possess fathomless skill. To mention him now was a small spark in the darkness – a spark of hope or a cruel taunt, Matajuro could not tell.

Lightning flashed once more, and Banzo's name seemed to hang in the charged air. Before Matajuro could respond, his father slid the shoji door closed behind him. The courtyard was empty except for Matajuro and the endless falling rain.

Matajuro remained kneeling in the mud long after his father departed. The storm raged on. The lantern flame finally guttered out, yielding the courtyard entirely to darkness. In the sky's repeated flares, he stared at the blade in his hand – its keen edge now trembling, its sheen dimmed by rainwater and dirt. The weight of it had never felt heavier.

Thunder growled in the distance as Matajuro struggled to his feet. Every muscle ached; every part of him was drenched and cold. Yet inside his chest, amidst the ashes of humiliation, his resolve flared anew. His father's words had been final, but Matajuro's ambition was not extinguished – not tonight, not ever.

He lifted his katana and slid it back into its scabbard. The sound of the steel finding home was soft against the roar of rain, nearly lost, but to Matajuro it felt like a promise.

Hands shaking, he bowed toward the darkened house – a gesture of respect and farewell to his father, who he knew watched unseen from behind the paper walls. Then Matajuro turned on his heel and walked out of the courtyard gate, rainwater coursing off his sleeves and pooling around his feet.

At the gate's threshold, he paused and looked back one last time through the curtain of rain. Lightning illuminated the yard he was leaving – the only home he had ever known, now as distant as a memory. He lowered his head and whispered a hoarse vow into the storm: "I will become a master swordsman... whatever it takes."

As Matajuro stepped beyond the gate, the night closed around him. The rain continued to fall, erasing his footprints in the mud. The blade at his side was silent, but with each step forward, he felt its presence – a reminder of what he must become. He disappeared into darkness, carrying only his sword, his unyielding ambition, and the name of a mountain swordsman echoing in his mind.

Banzo. The journey had begun.

PART I – ASHES AND AMBITION

Only when pride is reduced to ashes can determination be forged from its embers.

Dawn found Matajuro still on the road, clothes damp and heart heavy. The storm had blown itself out in the night, leaving behind tatters of mist that clung to the roadside pines. He trudged onward beneath dripping branches, each footstep squelching on the softened earth. In the east, a pale sun struggled to penetrate the morning haze, its light turning the lingering rainwater on the leaves into glistening beads. Matajuro's legs were leaden with exhaustion, but he refused to rest. Not now. He had a destination: Mount Futara, where the swordsman Banzo was said to live in seclusion.

For two days and nights, Matajuro had traveled with scarcely a pause. He had left his father's estate with nothing more than a small bundle of clothes and a pouch of cold rice. Now the rice was gone, and weariness gnawed at his limbs, yet he pressed on, fueled by the ember of determination that refused to die within him. Whenever his resolve wavered, he recalled the look in his father's eyes beneath the rain – that mix of disappointment and finality – and it steeled him anew. He would climb the mountain and find Banzo. He would beg the old master to teach him, to shape him into the swordsman his father believed he could never become.

By midday, the clouds had scattered, revealing a wide blue sky. The mountain path grew steeper, winding through cedars and ancient boulders coated in moss. The forest was hushed save for the gentle sigh of wind through the treetops and the distant trickle of unseen streams. Matajuro's stomach clenched with hunger, but he ignored it. He paused by a clear stream to drink and splash water on his face. The cold mountain water refreshed him and sharpened his mind. Kneeling there, he allowed himself a moment to take in the surroundings: the solitude of the peaks, the clean scent of wet pine needles, the play of sunlight on the running water.

In that quiet, Matajuro realized how far he had come – not just in distance, but from the world he knew. Down below lay the realm of lords and samurai, of his family name and its expectations. Up here, he was nameless, just another traveler on a narrow path. A sense of both fear and freedom washed over him. He was alone with his ambition and the daunting task ahead. If Banzo refused him... Matajuro clenched a fist, scattering droplets from his wet sleeves. No, he could not allow that to happen. He had nothing to return to; failure was unthinkable.

As the sun dipped toward afternoon, he came upon a small village clinging to the mountainside – scarcely more than a handful of wooden huts and terraced fields. Surprised to find any settlement this high up, Matajuro entered quietly, bowing in greeting to an old farmer leading an ox along the road. The farmer nodded back, eyeing the stranger's sword and travel-worn appearance with curiosity but no hostility.

Matajuro dared to ask, voice hoarse from hours of silence, "Honored sir, is this the way to Master Banzo's dwelling?"

The farmer stopped, squinting at Matajuro beneath his straw hat. He let out a dry chuckle. "Banzo?

The swordsman? Aye, he lives further up, near the summit." The old man pointed with a gnarled finger toward a forested ridge looming above the village. "Follow the footpath beyond our fields. You'll find a torii gate and a stone stair. His hut's at the end of it."

Matajuro bowed deeply. "Thank you."

The farmer hesitated, then added, "Many seek out Master Banzo. Few return as they expect."

Matajuro felt his pulse quicken. "What do you mean?"

The old man smiled thinly. "He's a difficult one, they say. Tests the mettle of those who come banging on his door." The farmer shrugged as if it were no concern of his and tugged the ox's rope. "Good luck, young swordsman. You might be needing it." With that and a nod, the farmer continued on his way, leaving Matajuro alone on the path.

Matajuro took a steadying breath and pressed on through the village. Past the last modest house and its vegetable plot, he found the footpath the farmer had described. It narrowed and snaked upward into a dense grove of cedar and cypress. Gnarled roots twisted across the trail, and patches of mist drifted between the trunks, cool against Matajuro's face.

Soon he spied the torii gate – two weathered wooden pillars supporting a crossbeam – standing silently among the trees. Its once-bright vermilion paint had flaked away, leaving it mottled and almost absorbed by the forest. Weeds grew at its base, and a paper strand of old prayers fluttered from one side. Matajuro passed beneath the gate, feeling a flutter in his chest. This was the threshold to Banzo's domain. He knew that in Shinto belief, a torii marked sacred ground, a place of gods or spirits. Here it seemed to mark the entrance to another kind of sanctum – that of a master who could decide Matajuro's fate with a single word.

Beyond the torii, stone steps led upward, half-buried under fallen leaves. Matajuro ascended, heart thumping louder with each step. After a short but steep climb, the forest opened into a small clearing. There, perched on the mountainside, stood a simple hut with a thatched roof and walls of gray wood. Next to it, a narrow garden lay tidy despite the wildness of the surrounding woods, with neat rows of vegetables and a small cherry tree now bare of leaves as autumn deepened. Nearby, a large flat rock overlooked a vista of distant foothills and sky.

Matajuro paused at the edge of the clearing, wiping sweat from his palms onto his damp kimono. No movement came from the hut. A curl of smoke from a thin bamboo pipe on the roof told him a fire burned inside. He stepped forward, unsure whether to call out. His voice faltered in his throat.

Instead, he approached the hut's door and knelt respectfully on the ground outside it. He set down his bundle and placed his hands on his thighs, waiting in silence. His heart hammered as minutes passed. The only sounds were the soft sigh of mountain wind and the caw of a distant crow.

At last, Matajuro cleared his throat and spoke, keeping his tone polite but loud enough to be heard through the paper-paneled door. "Master Banzo," he said, hoping he assumed correctly that the occupant was indeed the man he sought. "I am Matajuro, son of Yagyu Tajima-no-kami. I have come to humbly request your instruction in swordsmanship."

Silence answered him. Matajuro listened intently. He thought he had heard, just for an instant, a slight rustling within, but now there was nothing. He remained kneeling, forcing patience into his shaking limbs. The afternoon sun angled through the cedar branches, casting lattice shadows on the ground. A few heartbeats more, and he tried again, raising his voice a little over the sigh of the breeze.

"Master Banzo," he called, "I beg you, please allow me to become your student. I will do anything required to learn from you."

This time, distinct footsteps creaked on the floorboards within. Matajuro's pulse quickened. The wooden door slid open partway with a jolt. In the dim interior, an imposing figure stood looking out at the kneeling youth.

Banzo was not as old as Matajuro had imagined from the legends. Perhaps in his late fifties, he had a sturdy build and carried himself with an effortless balance that Matajuro's trained eye did not miss. His hair was streaked with iron gray and pulled into a loose tail. A short, neatly trimmed beard framed a mouth set in a neutral line. But it was the man's eyes that struck Matajuro most – dark, piercing eyes, keen as a hawk's. They seemed to hold a deep, probing intelligence, and at the moment, a hint of wry curiosity as they took in Matajuro's soggy, disheveled state.

Banzo said nothing at first, letting the silence and his unblinking stare unnerve the boy. Matajuro held his bowing posture, head lowered, though he dared a glance up to show his sincerity. The master's attire was plain – a faded indigo kimono and rough trousers. In one hand he held a ladle, as if interrupted from some household chore. The aroma of miso and smoke drifted out – he might have been tending a cooking pot.

At length, Banzo spoke, his voice low and unexpectedly gentle. "The son of Yagyu Tajima-no-kami, you say." He looked Matajuro over, eyebrow slightly raised. "Why is the son of so famed a swordsman kneeling at my door, asking instruction? Should you not be learning from your own father?"

Matajuro felt a flush of shame heat his face despite the chill. He pressed his forehead to the wooden threshold. "My father has cast me out," he said quietly. "He... he believes I lack the skill to become a master under his teaching." Saying it aloud tightened a painful knot in Matajuro's chest. But he forced himself to continue steadily, "He told me to seek you, Master Banzo. I beg you, take me as your student. I will devote my life to learning your swordsmanship."

Banzo was silent. Matajuro could only hear the pounding of his own heart and the distant cry of that crow circling in the sky. At last the master released a slow exhale through his nose.

"You wish to learn swordsmanship under my guidance?" Banzo asked, as if reconfirming a trivial matter. "Stand up."

Matajuro obeyed, rising to his feet. His legs trembled from exhaustion and nerves, but he stood straight and met Banzo's gaze. The older man stepped out of the hut, sliding the door shut behind him.

Up close, Banzo was only a few inches taller than Matajuro, but he emanated an aura of grounded confidence that made him seem larger. Matajuro realized he was instinctively holding his breath as he awaited the master's verdict.

Banzo's eyes narrowed. "Tell me, boy. How long have you practiced sword?"

"Since I was a child, Master," Matajuro replied. "Nearly fifteen years."

A ghost of a frown crossed Banzo's face. "Fifteen years, and Tajima-no-kami found you unworthy of succession?"

Matajuro flinched internally at the bluntness. He bowed his head. "Yes. He said my technique was mediocre."

Banzo snorted softly – whether in agreement or sympathy, Matajuro could not tell. The master began to walk slowly around the youth, as if appraising a horse or an ox. Matajuro remained still, eyes forward, resisting the urge to track Banzo's movements with his head. He felt the older man's gaze like a weight on his shoulders and the back of his neck.

"You have your father's build," Banzo commented quietly from behind him. "And I see some calluses on your hands – you've worked hard at sword drills, no doubt. Show me your draw."

Matajuro's breath caught. Was this a test? He placed a hand on his katana's hilt and one on the scabbard, adopting the ready stance he had practiced countless times. In one fluid motion, he drew the blade, slicing the air in front of him with a controlled horizontal cut. The steel gleamed in the afternoon light as droplets of condensation flicked off its length.

Banzo watched from the side, arms folded. The strike had been crisp, and Matajuro felt a small surge of confidence at performing a familiar motion well. But Banzo's face remained impassive. He stepped forward and, without a word, reached out. His hand wrapped around Matajuro's sword arm just above the wrist. Matajuro froze. The old master's grip was firm like iron.

Without warning, Banzo jerked Matajuro's arm, sending a jolt through him. With Banzo's other hand, he tapped the flat of Matajuro's blade, still extended in the finishing position of the cut. The sword vibrated from the tap, a low hum.

"Off-balance," Banzo said curtly.

Matajuro's cheeks burned. He realized his stance had faltered just slightly when Banzo pulled him – enough for his blade to waver and hum. He recovered and stepped back, lowering his sword. A moment ago he had been confident in his form; now he felt like a child caught playing with a weapon beyond his ability.

Banzo released him and stepped back, scratching his chin. "Your father was correct," he said simply. "You cannot fulfill the requirements to master the sword."

It was the very judgment Matajuro had dreaded. Coming from Banzo's mouth it felt like a door slamming shut. For a heartbeat, he stood motionless, stunned by how swiftly hope was slipping away.

Banzo turned as if to return to his hut, as though the matter were settled. Panic flared in Matajuro's chest. He fell to his knees, catching the master's sleeve with his free hand, his sword still clutched in the other.

"Master, please!" Matajuro's voice cracked with urgency. "If I lack skill now, I will train twice as hard. I will endure any hardship. Just... please do not send me away."

Banzo paused and looked down at the young man gripping his sleeve. The master's expression was unreadable, but he did not pull away. Matajuro pressed his forehead nearly to the dirt, swallowing his pride entirely. "I have no other path," he said, voice thick. "Let me stay as your disciple. Test me as you will. If I fail, you can cast me out then – but give me a chance to prove I can learn."

Slowly, Banzo tugged his sleeve free from Matajuro's grasp. The desperation in Matajuro's plea hung in the air. The older man studied the kneeling youth for a long moment, arms folded within his sleeves. Matajuro kept his eyes on the ground, chest heaving with emotion and exhaustion.

After what felt like an eternity, Banzo spoke again, his tone flat. "How keen are you to become a master swordsman, truly?"

Matajuro raised his head slightly. "It is my only desire, Master. My deepest ambition."

Banzo tilted his head. "If I were to take you on... if," he emphasized, "how many years do you imagine it will take for you to achieve master-level skill under me?"

Matajuro blinked, unsure if this meant Banzo was considering his request. He must answer carefully. "I am willing to devote my whole life," he said, repeating what he had vowed. "However long it takes."

Banzo gave a small snort. "Your whole life. Hmph. That is how long it would take – the rest of your life."

Matajuro's heart skipped. Was that a refusal or a literal estimate? The rest of his life could mean forever, an unreachable goal. He tried to clarify, voice hushed, "If I train diligently, Master... surely there must be some estimate. Ten years, perhaps?"

At this, Banzo raised an eyebrow. "Ten years? For mastership?"

Matajuro licked his dry lips. "I... I was thinking if I work extremely hard, day and night, maybe I could shorten it. My father..." he hesitated, "My father is growing old. Soon I will need to show him my skill, to care for him in his final years." The words tumbled out, half-truth and half a lingering hope that he might reconcile with his father one day. "I cannot spend my entire life as an apprentice. Please, Master Banzo, if I put forth double effort, from dawn until midnight each day – how long might it be before I am as good as any samurai in the land?"

Banzo's eyes glinted with something like amusement, though his voice stayed dry. "If you train day and night with all your might... then it will take you thirty years."

Matajuro looked up in shock. Thirty? He must have misheard. "Thirty years?" he repeated incredulously. "Master, you said ten years if I'm merely devoted. Why would training twice as hard double the time?"

Banzo's face broke into the faintest of smiles, though it did not reach his eyes. "Young man, if you have one eye fixed on the goal, you have only one eye left to guide you on the path." He shook his head. "A man in such a hurry as you seldom learns quickly."

Matajuro flushed, realizing the rebuke. His initial impulse to argue died on his tongue. Banzo had seen straight through him. Every part of him yearned to prove himself swiftly – to show his father he wasn't a failure, to reclaim his honor. But Banzo regarded that very urgency as a hindrance.

Shame and resolve warred within Matajuro. Slowly, he bowed until his forehead touched the ground again. "Forgive my impatience, Master," he said quietly. The damp earth cooled his skin. "I understand. I only asked out of concern for my father. But you are right – I must not rush."

He lifted his head and met Banzo's gaze with newfound steadiness. "I will do as you say, no matter how long it takes. If it takes the rest of my life, so be it. I will remain here and learn from you, Master Banzo, for as many years as necessary."

The sincerity in Matajuro's voice lingered in the clear mountain air. Banzo searched the youth's face for any insincerity or wavering. Finding none, he gave a single nod.

"Very well," Banzo said quietly. "If you agree to that, you may stay."

Relief and gratitude surged in Matajuro's chest so

strongly that he had to restrain himself from bowing repeatedly or even weeping. He pressed his palms to the ground and bowed low one last time. "Thank you, Master," he whispered.

Banzo turned and slid open the door of his hut. He gestured with a tilt of his head for Matajuro to enter. Matajuro quickly wiped his damp eyes and rose, sheathing his sword before stepping inside.

The hut's interior was dim but neat. A small hearth smoldered in the center, its smoke funneling through the roof pipe he'd seen outside. Beside it sat a cast iron pot emitting the savory scent of miso soup. A single straw mat was rolled up in the corner, and shelves along one wall held a sparse collection of items: a few clay bowls, some scrolls, a whetstone, a set of neatly coiled ropes, and on the highest shelf, a single katana in its scabbard, resting on a wooden rack. The sword's presence was subtle yet commanding, like a silent guardian of the space.

Matajuro glanced at the sheathed katana on the rack – could that be Banzo's famous blade? Before he could dwell on it, Banzo cleared his throat.

"You may sleep there," the master said, pointing to a corner where a second straw mat lay folded. "And put your things beside it. There is water in the urn outside if you need to wash."

KEVIN L. MICHEL

Matajuro moved to where indicated and set down his bundle and sword, feeling suddenly awkward and out of place. The reality of his new life here was settling in – a life that, for now, consisted of this one-room hut and a taciturn master watching him with evaluating eyes.

Banzo ladled out two bowls of soup from the pot and handed one to Matajuro. Gratefully, Matajuro accepted. The broth was plain and a bit watery, with a few floating bits of root vegetable, but to Matajuro's hunger it tasted like a feast. He savored each sip, conscious that Banzo ate silently across from him.

When they finished, Banzo spoke, each word deliberate. "From this day on, you are my apprentice. But you will not speak of swordsmanship. You will not ask me to teach technique."

Matajuro looked at him in surprise, but Banzo's face offered no explanation. The master continued, "You will do as I say and keep to the tasks I give you until I judge the time is right. Do you accept this?"

Matajuro set down his bowl and bowed his head. "Yes, Master. I will do whatever you ask."

Banzo nodded, satisfied. "Good. Then listen well. At dawn each day, you will rise and fetch water from the stream yonder." He gestured vaguely beyond the hut. "Fill the barrel by the door. After that, you will

24

prepare the morning rice. I trust you know how to cook rice?"

"Yes," Matajuro answered. In truth, as a lord's son he had rarely cooked, but he had observed servants enough to manage something as basic as rice.

"You will tend the garden – weed it, water it – and gather vegetables as needed. There is an axe by the woodpile; you will split firewood for our hearth. You will also keep this hut clean, sweep the floors, dust the shelves." Banzo's dark eyes fixed on Matajuro. "These tasks are now your training."

Each chore Banzo listed dropped into Matajuro's gut like a stone. Water? Firewood? He had anticipated hardship, yes, but he had imagined sword drills from dawn to dusk, punishing sparring matches, long meditations on technique – not... household chores. Was this a joke? But Banzo's expression remained serious.

A flicker of indignation sparked in Matajuro's chest, quickly smothered by caution. This must be another test, he reasoned. Perhaps Banzo wanted to see if he would complain. Matajuro bowed. "I understand, Master. I will do all that you have said."

Banzo gave the slightest hint of a smile at the corners of his mouth. "We shall see," he said softly.

That evening, Matajuro scrubbed the soup bowls

clean and stepped outside to empty the water. The sun had set and the mountain air was biting cold. Above, a spray of stars shimmered in a moonless sky. He looked out over the dark silhouettes of the valleys below. Tiny pinpricks of light glowed from the village and farther beyond, perhaps the towns near his former home.

He wondered what his father was doing at that moment – if he thought of his son now wandering beyond the family's reach, or if he had already put Matajuro out of mind entirely. The pain of that thought was still raw, but Matajuro steadied himself with a long breath of pine-scented air. He was here, under Banzo's roof, because he chose this path. His old life had burned to ashes behind him; ahead, only the uncertain path of ambition stretched out.

Matajuro looked down at his hands in the starlight. They were already roughened and dirty from just the small tasks done today. Fine lessons of swordplay and noble comforts were nowhere to be found here. A lesser resolve might crack in the face of this reality. But Matajuro felt a steely thread of determination weaving through his fatigue. He reminded himself: he had pledged to endure whatever Banzo demanded, for as long as it took.

He would meet each day's labor without complaint

and prove himself worthy of real instruction. And if that instruction was slow to come, he would wait. No matter if it was ten years or thirty or the rest of his life – he would wait.

With a final glance at the sky, Matajuro re-entered the hut and laid down on the straw mat that was now his bed. The floor was hard beneath it, and the mountain night was silent save for the faint chirring of crickets outside the walls. Banzo had already stretched out on his own mat, back turned, seemingly indifferent. Matajuro closed his eyes. His body was weary, but his mind churned with questions and hopes for the future. He forced himself to listen to the quiet around him – the crackle of the dying embers in the hearth, the sigh of wind slipping through the cracks. In that stillness, he said a silent prayer of thanks and resolve.

Thus, Matajuro's first day under Master Banzo's roof ended not with a sword in his hand, but a broom and a cookpot. Ashes and ambition – one life burned away, and another begun on this remote mountainside. As he drifted into a tentative sleep, Matajuro did not yet grasp how profoundly this simple life would change him. But he held firm to the one thing he could control: the promise he made to himself to persevere. In the darkness behind his

eyelids, the image of his sword flashed in his mind –
bright and sharp – and then faded into the quiet of a
long night, waiting for dawn.

PART II – YEARS WITHOUT STEEL

Through years without steel, the true blade is forged within.

Dawn light seeped pale and blue into the one-room hut as Matajuro rose quietly from his mat. He wrapped his thin cotton robe tighter against the pre-dawn chill. In the corner, Banzo still lay asleep, his form blanketed and unmoving except for the slow, steady rhythm of breath. Matajuro moved carefully so as not to wake the master, though by now he suspected Banzo woke or slept exactly as he intended, not at the whim of noise.

Stepping outside, Matajuro found the world still

cloaked in the last shreds of night. Over the eastern horizon, a faint glow heralded the coming sun. The air smelled of damp earth and cedar. He took the wooden bucket by the door and made his way down the narrow path toward the stream that gurgled down the mountainside. It was a walk he could do now almost blindfolded, his feet knowing each twist of the trail and each root that tried to snare an unwary toe.

At the stream's edge, Matajuro knelt and submerged the bucket, watching it fill. The water was icy; it bit at his skin and snapped him fully awake. As he hauled the bucket out, arms straining, the first bird calls of morning sounded in the trees. Droplets splashed onto his calves, but he paid no mind. A year ago, he might have shivered at the cold or grumbled inwardly at the weight—now it was simply the start of another day.

Back at the hut, he emptied the bucket into the large wooden barrel that stood under the eaves. A cloud of his breath hung in the air. Autumn was giving way to winter once more. He remembered arriving here in autumn, nearly three years past. Then, he had been brimming with eagerness despite exhaustion. He had imagined by this time he would be deep into mastering secret techniques of the sword. Instead, he found himself a practitioner of simpler arts: drawing water, tending fire, stirring miso broth.

Matajuro set the rice pot over the coals, added water from the barrel and a scoop of rice, and began to cook the morning meal. As the fire crackled softly, he quietly slid open the small window shutter to let in a bit of fresh air. Outside, the forest was transitioning from blue dawn to gold, trunks of trees emerging from night's obscurity. A light wind murmured, rattling the last dry leaves.

By the time Banzo rose and emerged from his blankets, the rice porridge was nearly ready. Matajuro bowed in greeting. Banzo offered a brief nod and a grunt of acknowledgment – which, from him, was a rather standard morning exchange. In silence, Matajuro served two bowls. Master and apprentice sat across from each other on the floor, neither speaking a word as they ate. The only sounds were the crackle of the fire and the soft scrape of wood against clay as Matajuro stirred the pot to prevent burning.

This wordless routine had become comfortable in its own way. In the beginning, the silence had unsettled Matajuro; he used to steal glances at Banzo, wondering what the master was thinking, whether he approved or disapproved of Matajuro's efforts.

Now he simply focused on eating mindfully. The hot rice warmed him from within, providing energy for the labor to come.

When Banzo finished, Matajuro did as every morning: he took the master's empty bowl and his own, rinsed them clean, and set them to dry. Banzo stood, stretched his arms, and without a word, left the hut. Matajuro watched the master wander off toward the forest edge where the morning light slanted through the pines. Banzo often took solitary walks after breakfast, sometimes carrying a small sickle to trim wild herbs or check his snares for rabbits. This too was part of the rhythm of life on the mountain.

Matajuro did not idle when Banzo was away. He had his orders and he kept to them diligently. Fetch water, make meals, tend the garden, chop wood, clean the hut – the tasks circled around each day like the turning of a wheel. Some days brought extra duties: repairing a leak in the roof after a heavy rain, carrying supplies up from the village, or helping the villagers plant or harvest in the terraced fields below. Banzo never gave these tasks as explicit training, but Matajuro approached them with the same determination he would approach a sword drill, pouring his energy into doing them well.

That morning, after washing up, Matajuro headed to the small garden patch. The winter vegetables – daikon radishes and hardy greens – needed checking. Kneeling in the moist soil, he pulled up a few stubborn weeds that had sprouted at the garden's edge. Each weed came up with a satisfying tug, roots clinging to dark clumps of earth. As he worked, the rising sun sent light glistening across dew drops on the broad radish leaves. Matajuro paused for a moment, the weed in his hand, and allowed himself to appreciate the beauty of it: tiny worlds reflected in each droplet, the quiet persistence of plants growing as seasons turned. He found that such moments of stillness came more frequently to him now.

In his early days here, Matajuro's mind would race constantly – fretting over how and when his training would begin in earnest, replaying the duel with his father in his head, fantasizing about future glory. But the mountain had a way of clearing those clouds of thought. Work and the endless presence of nature gradually emptied his mind of its anxious chatter. More and more, he lived in the present moment – the weight of a bucket in his hands, the texture of rough wood beneath the plane of a saw, the taste of simple food after hours of labor.

Still, a part of him quietly yearned. Some evenings,

after Banzo had retired, Matajuro would sit outside on that flat rock overlooking the dark valleys. There, under the pinprick stars, he would unsheathe his own katana from its storage cloth and examine it by starlight. He took care to keep the blade free of rust, wiping it with oil he'd traded from the village and sharpening it on Banzo's whetstone when he was certain the master was away. He did this not in defiance, but out of reverence for the weapon that symbolized his goal. Though he had sworn not to wield or mention the sword, he could not bear the thought of letting his treasured blade decay. So, in secret, he maintained it, even as he did not dare to practice cuts or forms.

Time flowed like the mountain stream, at times swift in its passing and at times agonizingly slow. Summer followed spring, and Matajuro toiled under the sun's heat, sweat soaking his robes as he split logs and hauled water for the thirsty garden. His skin browned, and his once smooth palms grew tough and calloused. On one sweltering afternoon, he chopped wood until his shoulders burned, swinging the axe in a steady rhythm. *Thunk!* The blade bit into cedar. *Crack!* Wood split and fell. His breaths found a pattern with the movements. He noticed that if he let tension go and swung with his whole body, the axe did the work almost on its own. The realization struck him oddly: he was improving at this mundane task, becoming more efficient, precise, and strong, just as he once improved at sword drills through repetition. The thought gave him a small surge of encouragement – perhaps, he mused, all this was indeed forging him in unexpected ways.

Banzo seldom commented on Matajuro's work. But occasionally, in the evening, the master would inspect the woodpile or the neatness of the hut and give a brief nod of approval. On a rare occasion, Matajuro thought he saw the slightest hint of a smile on Banzo's lips when tasting a particularly well-cooked meal of rice and wild greens. These small acknowledgments became treasured victories in Matajuro's heart, like glimpses of the sun through heavy clouds.

Yet, doubt was a weed that grew in the quiet of his mind. In the second year, as leaves fell for the second autumn in Matajuro's apprenticeship, a creeping fear began to take root: What if this was all he would ever do here? He had promised to be patient, but human hope is not easily quelled. Each night, lying on his straw mat, he grappled with uncertainty. Was he truly any closer to becoming a swordsman than when he'd arrived? His sword still sat untouched except for those secret maintenance rituals. Banzo had not so much as shown him a stance or a technique.

One evening, as the first winter snow dusted the ground outside, Matajuro finally dared to approach the subject – if only obliquely. He and Banzo sat by the hearth, the master whittling a piece of pine into a new garden stake and Matajuro mending a torn bit of fishing net. The silence between them was broken only by the pop of resin in the fire. Summoning his courage, Matajuro spoke without lifting his eyes from the net.

"Master," he said softly, "I am grateful for all that you have taught me."

Banzo's knife paused its carving for a fraction of a moment. "Mm," he grunted – an encouragement to continue, or just an acknowledgement.

Matajuro's hands tensed on the twine. "May I ask… have I been learning well?"

It was as far as he dared go towards the forbidden subject. His heart beat painfully, anticipating reprimand or a weighty silence.

Banzo set down the carved stake and blade. Matajuro could feel the master's gaze on him, though he kept his own eyes lowered. After a long moment, Banzo spoke calmly. "You have done all that I have asked of you."

Nothing more was said. The master picked up his knife and wood again, resuming the gentle scrape of carving. Matajuro swallowed a sigh. The indirect answer was clear: the topic of swordsmanship remained off-limits. And yet, Banzo's response held a note of truth – he had done everything asked. Perhaps that itself was the lesson: to do each thing fully without looking beyond. So Matajuro redoubled his resolve to give himself over to the tasks completely, and to trust in his teacher, however mysterious his methods.

Seasons turned again. The snows of winter melted into spring. Mountain cherry blossoms budded and burst into brief, radiant bloom around Banzo's hut. Matajuro found himself smiling at their arrival – he had grown fond of the cycles of nature which measured his time here. In spring, he helped Banzo plant new rows of vegetables, carefully pressing seeds into soil. "Not too deep," Banzo reminded quietly as they crouched side by side in the loamy earth. It was one of the few instructions Banzo had directly given in months. Matajuro adjusted his technique, feeling oddly pleased to receive even that small bit of guidance.

In summer, thunderstorms rolled across the peaks. One humid afternoon, clouds boiled black and the sky shook with thunder. Matajuro hurried to secure the tools and cover the woodpile as fat raindrops began to bombard the mountainside. The storm unleashed sheets of rain and wild wind that lashed the trees into a frenzy. Banzo's hut rattled, its paper windows bulging inwards with each gust. Matajuro rushed to reinforce a shutter, pushing it closed firmly just as a burst of wind nearly tore it off. In that flash, he realized Banzo stood at the other end of the room mirroring his action on another shutter. The master's movements were calm and unhurried, yet precise. They secured the hut with ropes and wooden braces to wait out the squall.

As they knelt by the firepit listening to the roar of wind, Banzo surprised Matajuro by speaking over the din. "In a storm, one can only secure what one can and let the rest be." His eyes watched the flickering flames, not the younger man. Matajuro wasn't entirely sure if Banzo was referring to more than just the shutters. Perhaps it was just an old man's comment on the weather. But Matajuro held onto those words nonetheless, turning them over in his mind. Secure what one can, and let the rest be. It sounded akin to something his father might have said about battle – control what you can; accept what you cannot.

Gradually the storm passed, leaving the world renewed and glistening. Matajuro stepped outside to assess the damage and saw that the garden had been battered but not destroyed, thanks in part to the stakes and twine he had helped put in place to support the plants. The air was cool and fresh, the frenzy of an hour ago replaced by dripping tranquility. Banzo came to stand beside him, hands tucked in his sleeves, surveying the clearing. Without turning, he said quietly, "Good work securing things." It was a simple acknowledgment, but Matajuro felt a glow of pride; praise from Banzo was as rare as finding a perfect pearl in a riverbed.

By the time the maple leaves blazed red and gold in the fourth autumn of Matajuro's apprenticeship, an observer might have mistaken him for a humble woodsman or farmer rather than a samurai's son. His once fine robes had long been replaced by sturdy work clothes, patched and stained from labor. His hair, now often tied up casually, had grown longer; he occasionally trimmed it with Banzo's knife to keep it out of the way. He had grown leaner but also stronger; carrying water and chopping wood had etched firm muscles on his arms and back. There was a quiet confidence in how he moved through the daily chores, a fluid economy of motion that Banzo noted silently.

And yet, for all the subtle transformations in his body and mind, Matajuro could not escape a growing melancholy that tugged at him whenever he remembered why he had come. He tried to keep such thoughts at bay, focusing instead on the present. But as the months rolled on with no sign of change in his training, a voice inside him whispered that perhaps his father had been right after all. Maybe Banzo never intended to truly train him – maybe this was all a way to let the years slip by until Matajuro gave up or grew old in obscurity.

One crisp evening, when the year's first frost silvered the garden rows, Matajuro found himself sitting on the threshold of the hut after supper, looking at the clear, cold stars. Banzo was inside, tending the hearth, the golden firelight spilling out around Matajuro's feet. In his hands, Matajuro absentmindedly turned a fallen maple leaf, red as a flame, now fading and dry. Three years, he thought. Three years gone.

He gazed at the sky, and for the first time in a long while, he let himself dwell on the past and future. He pictured his father's face, older and lined with concern or disappointment. Was his father even still alive and well? Had he heard any word of his son? Matajuro had sent no messages home; he had severed that connection to focus on his path here. But perhaps word had traveled that he was living as Banzo's helper. How would his father view that, if at all? Perhaps as an embarrassment, or perhaps he would simply scoff that Matajuro was doing a servant's work instead of becoming a warrior.

Matajuro closed his eyes. In these years, he had learned to quell frustration, but tonight sadness welled up unchecked. He felt at once very young and very foolish – a child who had run from home chasing a dream, only to find himself sweeping floors and washing rice bowls on a lonely mountain. A chill breeze whispered through the cedars, and Matajuro's eyes stung. He told himself it was the wind causing tears, but deep down he knew the truth: he was nearing a breaking point in the silence of his apprenticeship.

Behind him, Banzo's voice came softly from inside, interrupting his reverie. "It grows cold. Shut the door, will you?"

Matajuro hastily wiped his eyes with his sleeve and replied, "Yes, Master," hoping his voice betrayed nothing. He slid the door closed, shutting out the brilliant stars and the biting wind. The warmth of the hearth washed over him and he busied himself with stoking it for the night.

Banzo was already lying down, his back to the room. Matajuro lay on his own mat, but sleep did not come easily. He listened to the crickets chirping outside the window and the occasional sigh from Banzo as the older man drifted into sleep. In the darkness, Matajuro's doubts pressed heavily upon him. How much longer could he endure without any glimpse of the training he sought? Was he to spend the best years of his life as nothing more than Banzo's housekeeper?

Yet even as these questions plagued him, something deeper held him back from abandoning this path. A promise, like a thread of steel woven through his soul: the vow he'd made in that rain-soaked night to do whatever it took. If he left now, all those days of labor and patience would be meaningless, and worse, his father's judgment of him would be confirmed.

Matajuro inhaled slowly, filling his lungs with the cool night air seeping through the gaps in the wooden walls. He let the breath out, releasing some of the tension. He had come too far to give up. If there was a secret in this seemingly endless drudgery, he had yet to uncover it—but he would trust that no effort was truly wasted under Banzo's eye. He would continue to endure, if only for the sake of that spark of hope Banzo had kindled by agreeing to teach him at all.

Still, as he finally felt himself falling asleep, one last thought flickered in his mind: *How much longer?* The question hung in the silence, unanswered.

Unbeknownst to Matajuro, on his own mat Banzo lay awake a while longer, gaze fixed on the ceiling's darkness. The master's perceptive ears had not missed the soft tremor in his apprentice's voice earlier, nor the quiet sniff while Matajuro sat in the doorway. Banzo's keen eyes had observed the young man's growing melancholy in recent weeks – the way his usually steady focus sometimes drifted, the way he sighed when he believed no one could hear. Banzo stroked his beard thoughtfully. He had pushed Matajuro to the brink of despair by design, stretching the bowstring of the youth's spirit to its limits. Now, perhaps, it was nearly time to release it.

Banzo closed his eyes, a slight smile ghosting across his lips in the darkness. The true training was about to begin.

PART III – RAIN OF BLOWS

Steel is tempered into a sword only by enduring countless blows.

Matajuro awoke before dawn as usual, the chill of early morning clinging to his skin. He sat up on his mat and quietly rolled it away, careful not to make noise. Banzo's mat was already empty – not unusual, as the master sometimes rose even earlier for his solitary exercises or walks. Matajuro assumed Banzo had gone to relieve himself or gather kindling for the fire. Rubbing sleep from his eyes, Matajuro threw on his robe and stepped outside to begin his morning tasks.

A grey mist drifted among the pines, and the

ground was damp with dew. Matajuro moved towards the barrel to see if any water remained from yesterday. Without warning, a sharp whistle cut through the air behind him. Before he could fully turn, a crack exploded across his shoulders. Blinding pain shot down his back. Matajuro cried out and staggered, nearly dropping to his knees. The wooden bucket he had been reaching for toppled from its stand, water sloshing uselessly onto the dirt.

Heart pounding and breath seized in shock, Matajuro twisted around. Banzo stood just a few paces away, feet planted firmly, a stout wooden bokken (practice sword) in his hands. The mist swirled around the master's figure, giving him a phantom-like air. Matajuro's mind whirled in confusion. He opened his mouth to speak, but words failed him. His shoulders throbbed where the wooden blade had struck—surely a bruise was already blooming beneath his robe.

Banzo regarded him with calm indifference, lowering the bokken. The older man's voice, when it came, was utterly ordinary, as if nothing unusual had occurred. "You were not prepared," was all he said.

With that, Banzo turned on his heel and walked back toward the hut, leaving Matajuro standing dumbfounded in the damp yard, one hand gingerly pressed to his aching shoulder. The morning light was growing, the mists thinning, but to Matajuro it felt as though the world had tilted into some strange new orbit.

He could scarcely believe what had happened. In three years, Banzo had never so much as raised his voice to him—let alone a weapon. The wooden sword in Banzo's hand had appeared out of nowhere; Matajuro hadn't even known the master possessed one. The stinging pain was proof enough that it was no apparition. Banzo had deliberately struck him, hard and without warning.

At first, a flare of anger ignited in Matajuro's chest. Had he done something wrong to merit this? Or was Banzo simply taunting him, showing how easily he could be beaten? He recalled his father's disdainful words, the humiliation of defeat in the rain. Was this morning's blow a reminder of his incompetence?

But as Matajuro stood there, teeth clenched against the pain, a second realization dawned on him, smothering his anger and replacing it with a cautious hope. This had to be part of his training. Why else would Banzo strike him now, after so long? Perhaps at last the master was ready to teach, albeit in his own harsh way.

Matajuro inhaled slowly, steadying himself. If this

was training, he had to embrace it. He retrieved the fallen bucket, refilled it from the morning's fetch, and carried on with preparing the rice, despite the ache radiating from his upper back. When the breakfast was ready, he brought Banzo his bowl. Banzo sat on the porch, wooden sword resting casually across his lap as if it were a walking stick. Matajuro's eyes flicked to the weapon, then to Banzo's imperturbable face. The master met his gaze briefly, but said nothing about the incident. His expression revealed nothing —no anger, no jest, no explanation.

They ate in silence. Matajuro's mind raced behind his composed facade. He replayed the moment over and over, dissecting his own reactions. He had been utterly caught off guard. Banzo's approach had been silent, his strike swift and perfectly aimed. Matajuro had sensed nothing until the instant of impact. If that had been a real sword, he might be dead.

By the time he finished his bowl, Matajuro had made a decision: he would not allow himself to be taken by surprise again. If this was to be his training, he would meet it head on. He vowed silently to keep his awareness sharp every moment, to feel any hint of movement in the air behind him, to listen for the slightest rustle that could betray Banzo's presence.

That resolve was soon put to the test. Later that

morning, Matajuro was in the woods behind the hut, gathering kindling for the fire. The forest was quiet except for the chirp of waking birds and the crunch of twigs under his sandals. His shoulder still ached dully, but he forced himself to focus outward, straining to catch any irregular sound. At first, every rustle of leaves made his heart jump. He paused frequently, fingers tight around the bundle of sticks, eyes scanning the shadows. But he saw no sign of Banzo.

After collecting a decent armful of kindling, Matajuro started back toward the clearing. He stepped between two cedar trunks and . . . *whoosh* . . . the air behind him stirred. Matajuro flung himself forward instinctively. A wooden blade swiped just past his ear, close enough that he heard it whistle through the space his head had occupied a split-second before. He tumbled to the ground, scattering sticks everywhere.

Banzo's form materialized behind him, bokken mid-swing. The master's strike had missed by the slimmest margin, and only because Matajuro had flung himself flat. Matajuro scrambled up, breathing hard. Pine needles clung to his clothes. His hands shook slightly from the burst of adrenaline.

Banzo stood straight, lowering the bokken again. A

faint smile – or was it a shadow? – crossed his lips. He gave a curt nod, as if acknowledging that Matajuro had moved quicker this time. Then wordlessly, he bent down, picked up one of the dropped sticks, and tossed it back to Matajuro. The message was clear: continue your task... and stay alert.

Matajuro bowed quickly in acknowledgement, not trusting his voice to be steady. Banzo melted once more into the trees.

For the rest of that day, Matajuro lived on the balls of his feet, every muscle subtly tensed, every sense strained. It was exhausting. While stirring the simmering miso at midday, his ears were pricked for any footstep beyond the constant bubbling of the pot. While scrubbing laundry in the stream, his eyes kept darting to the ripples and reflections, half-expecting to see Banzo's form looming behind him in the water's mirror. Twice, he nearly jumped out of his skin at innocuous things – a squirrel skittering through fallen leaves; an acorn dropping onto a rock.

Yet, for all his vigilance, Banzo still found opportunities to strike. That evening, while Matajuro was bent over the garden, pruning the withered stems of summer's bean plants, the master appeared as silently as a fox. A sudden thwack on Matajuro's rear sent him sprawling face-first into the dirt.

Matajuro yelped more from surprise than pain, scrabbling around just in time to see the hem of Banzo's kimono disappear around the corner of the hut, a ghostly laugh hanging in the air. Cheeks burning with humiliation, Matajuro dusted himself off and realized he had loosened his focus for a mere breath, and Banzo had seized the moment.

That night, Matajuro collapsed onto his mat with his body battered and mind weary. Every part of him ached, shoulders, back, thighs. Aches reminding him of each attack he had failed to avoid. He lay awake long after Banzo's breathing had deepened into the cadence of sleep. Matajuro's own heartbeat thudded in his ears as he replayed the day's ambushes. Not a single moment felt safe now.

He realized that even here, in what should be the refuge of night, he could not fully relax. Banzo could, for all he knew, strike him in his sleep. The thought made him sit up and peer through the darkness towards Banzo's silhouette. The master was lying still. Was he truly asleep, or merely feigning, waiting for Matajuro to drop his guard? Matajuro's mind chased itself in circles. If he stayed awake all night, he'd be useless the next day. If he slept, he might be rudely awakened by a wooden sword to his ribs—or worse, to his skull.

Ultimately, exhaustion claimed him in the small hours, but it was a light and tormented sleep. He dreamed of walking through a field of tall grasses that hid stalking wolves; each time the grass rustled he would whirl, only to see nothing—until finally a grey shape lunged and he woke with a start, heart hammering.

In the dull predawn, Matajuro rose from his mat, feeling as though he had hardly rested at all. His nerves were taut wires. As he stepped out to fetch water, he clutched the bucket so tightly his knuckles whitened, eyes scanning every shadow among the trees.

Yet Banzo did not attack that morning. In fact, the master was nowhere to be seen. Matajuro carried on his chores under a cloud of anticipation, unsure when and where the next blow would fall. The emptiness of the morning path and the stillness of the hut pressed on him almost as heavily as Banzo's presence would have. Was the master watching from some hidden vantage, waiting for Matajuro to slip into complacency? Matajuro dared not assume otherwise.

He moved through each task deliberately, forcing himself not to rush in panic, but also not relaxing in the slightest. He felt a curious clarity amid the tension – each sound, each shift of light became vivid in his awareness. The buzz of a dragonfly's wings, the distant creak of a bending branch, the soft crunch of his own footsteps on gravel – all distinct, noted, yet allowed to pass without jarring him. He began to realize that if he let fear take over, he would be paralyzed; instead, he had to welcome the heightened state as a new way of being.

By afternoon, Banzo still had not shown himself. Matajuro began to wonder if the previous day had been a one-time ordeal. Perhaps Banzo considered the lesson finished? Or was this a deeper test – lulling him into doubt or a false sense of security before striking again?

The answer came soon enough. Matajuro was kneeling by the stream scrubbing a pair of Banzo's mud-stained trousers on a washboard. The sun was warm and cicadas droned in the grasses. The rhythmic work and the gentle murmur of water almost made him forget his caution—almost. But some inner signal, a prickle at the back of his neck, made Matajuro pause. The cicadas had abruptly fallen silent. A breath of wind against his cheek hinted at movement behind him. Without hesitating, Matajuro threw himself to one side, rolling in the pebbled shallows of the stream.

A split second later, splash! Banzo's wooden sword

sliced into the water where Matajuro had been. A spray of cold stream water showered Matajuro as he scrambled up the opposite bank, panting. He stood drenched but unharmed, the chill of the water sharpening his senses further.

Banzo straightened from his failed strike, water dripping from the bokken. His sandals were submerged in the stream's flow. Matajuro stood across from him, chest heaving, soaked laundry forgotten. They locked eyes. Banzo's face remained stern, but there was a brightness in his eyes—a glint of approval perhaps.

Matajuro could not help a small smile of triumph from tugging at his lips. He had evaded this one— barely, but it counted. He bowed across the stream, never taking his eyes off the master. Banzo gave the slightest incline of his head in return. Then, to Matajuro's astonishment, the older man let out a short laugh, as rare and fleeting as a fox's bark. Not a mocking laugh, but something like satisfaction.

"Finish the washing," Banzo said calmly, stepping out of the water. He flicked the bokken to shed droplets, then tucked it under his arm as he might a walking cane. As he passed by, he added in a quiet tone, "Better—but not enough. Do not lose focus." The words were offered almost kindly.

Matajuro nodded, heart still pounding, and watched Banzo depart up the path, water trailing from the master's clothes.

In the following days, the attacks continued—and escalated. Banzo struck at any and every time: midday, midnight, during work, during meals, even in the midst of conversation (though conversations themselves were few). If Matajuro let his attention waver for even an instant, the bokken would find its mark. A jab to the ribs while he hung laundry on the line; a swipe at his ankles as he stepped over the threshold; an overhead crack aimed at his head as he bent to pick vegetables (that one caught him glancingly and left a painful lump). Banzo was tireless and unpredictable, a shadow with a wooden blade.

Matajuro developed a collection of bruises of every size—bluish splotches on his arms, thighs, and backside; tender spots on his shoulders and calves. His hands, often flung up in frantic defense, became calloused in new places and sometimes bled from grazing the bokken's wooden edge. Yet he persisted. Though each stinging strike tested his resolve, he treated them as fuel for his determination. Each failure to dodge or block became a lesson seared into muscle and bone.

And gradually—imperceptibly at first—Matajuro improved. What began as clumsy, panicked flailing transformed slowly into smoother, more instinctive reactions. He learned to trust his peripheral vision, catching sight of the slightest motion at the edges of his awareness. His hearing attuned to Banzo's presence in subtle ways: the soft crunch of a leaf, the faint displacement of air, the way birds quieted and insects paused when the master was stalking near.

There were moments when Matajuro could almost sense Banzo's intent, as though an invisible ripple preceded the master's physical arrival. In those moments, Matajuro's body would move before thought—flinching or ducking or twisting away in a reflex born of countless close calls. Sometimes, to his own surprise, he even managed to counter in small ways: swinging a laundry pole between himself and an incoming strike to deflect it, or kicking over a stool in Banzo's path to hinder the pursuit.

Such successes were still rare, but when they occurred, Matajuro felt a quiet exhilaration bloom in his chest. It was not pride exactly—more a growing confidence in abilities he didn't know he had. After one particularly deft evasion—he had somersaulted over the woodpile to avoid a sweeping low strike, leaving Banzo momentarily on the other side of the stack—the master had actually paused to laugh out loud. It was a rich, genuine laugh that startled Matajuro nearly as much as the attack. Banzo had then clapped him on the shoulder (nearly as hard as a blow) and said, "You've turned into a squirrel, boy!" before wandering off, leaving Matajuro catching his breath and smiling despite a scraped knee.

With each day, Matajuro found he could endure more. The initial fear that spiked through him at each ambush gradually settled into a steady vigilance that no longer paralyzed him. His sleep, while still light, became more restful as his subconscious mind adjusted to the constant demand. He began to wake even at the faintest creak of the hut's floorboards, sometimes catching Banzo's silhouette in the act of looming over him in the dark. On one occasion, Matajuro woke just as Banzo was raising the bokken above his blanketed form; Matajuro rolled off his mat in a heartbeat, hearing the wooden sword thud into the floor where he'd lain. Banzo had grunted in surprise, and Matajuro scrambled to his feet with a grin of triumph even in the blackness. He knew Banzo could sense his smile. The master merely chuckled and whispered, "Go back to sleep," before slipping outside like a phantom.

The mountain life took on a new rhythm—a

relentless dance of hunter and prey, except the prey was becoming agile and aware. Matajuro's chores continued, but they were now interwoven with an ever-present readiness, like a second heartbeat. Washing clothes was also training his reflexes; chopping vegetables honed his alertness as much as it did his knife skills, for at any moment Banzo might dart in through the door with a wooden strike.

Despite the ceaseless tension, Matajuro felt more alive than he ever had. Each successfully dodged blow was a thrill, each near miss a motivator, each bruise a badge of instruction. Banzo's training was brutal and wordless, but Matajuro began to understand its language. He was being taught not through theory or kata, but through survival – through living on the edge of a wooden sword, day in and day out.

As the late summer rolled into autumn once more, the leaves on the mountain began to turn fiery hues and the morning air gained a crisp bite. It had been months since that first strike at dawn. Matajuro, now in the thick of this trial by fire, had transformed in ways he could not have previously fathomed. He moved through his day with a catlike grace, taut but flowing, always poised to spring aside or counter. His eyes, once dreamy with distant ambition or clouded with doubt, now held a steady focus, scanning and absorbing his surroundings with clarity and calm.

Yet he knew he was not perfect. Banzo still managed to catch him off guard at times, especially when devising new ploys. Only yesterday, the master had feigned an injury, groaning and calling for help from behind the hut; when Matajuro rushed over in concern, Banzo sprang up from the ground and nearly whacked him on the forehead. Matajuro barely pulled back in time, falling flat to avoid the swing, and earned a scolding: "Never assume the enemy is weak." Chastened, Matajuro bowed deeply in apology, even as he silently marveled at the lesson's cunning.

The "rain of blows" that Banzo unleashed was not merely physical; it was an unending mental puzzle, a wordless riddle in action. There was no pattern to memorize, no form to rehearse—only pure reaction and presence. Matajuro had no choice but to abandon any pretense or planning; he lived fully in the present, responding purely to what each moment brought. In doing so, he found a kind of freedom. The worries about tomorrow or regrets of yesterday had no space in a mind that had to remain as clear and empty as a cloudless sky, open to any possibility.

One evening, as Matajuro prepared the fire for supper, he noticed Banzo watching him quietly from just beyond the threshold. The master leaned on the bokken like a cane, but made no move to strike. Instead, he spoke in a low voice, almost more to the fire than to Matajuro, "Do you know, Matajuro, how a hawk survives in the wild?"

Matajuro looked up, surprised that Banzo had initiated conversation unprompted. He considered for a moment. This felt like another test, but a different kind. "A hawk must always be alert, Master," he answered slowly. "It soars high but watches the ground keenly for any movement. It doesn't relax even when gliding."

Banzo nodded, the firelight etching lines of approval on his face. "Just so. If it loses focus, even for a breath, it may miss its prey—or become prey to another."

Matajuro met Banzo's eyes. He sensed the double meaning. "I understand."

Banzo grunted softly, satisfied. He did not raise the wooden sword at all that night, allowing Matajuro a rare evening of peace by the hearth—though Matajuro's guard remained up, just in case.

As they ate their simple meal, Matajuro felt a swell of gratitude amid his weariness. Banzo's methods were severe, even cruel at times, but they were working. Matajuro could feel it in the quickness of his limbs, the quietness of his mind, the way his awareness had expanded to embrace the whole environment. He thought of an old saying he had heard in childhood: "The sword is more than a weapon; it is an extension of one's body and spirit." He had always thought that meant practicing forms with a blade in hand. Now, he suspected he understood it on a deeper level—his body and spirit were being forged into a living weapon even without a sword physically present. His very being was learning to behave like a drawn blade: poised, balanced, and razor-sharp in attention.

That night, as Matajuro lay down to rest, bruised but content, he realized something startling. He could not recall the last time he had thought about when his training would "truly begin." It was obvious now that it had begun long ago—and he was in the midst of it, surviving it, growing through it. The ambition that once had gnawed at him had been transmuted into the simple will to meet each moment correctly. Master Banzo had given him the greatest gift by giving him nothing except the need to discover his own strength.

Matajuro closed his eyes. Outside, a gentle autumn rain began to patter on the thatched roof, a soothing rhythm. For a brief moment, anxiety crept in—rain might mask Banzo's approach, making it harder to hear. But then Matajuro let the thought go. It didn't matter. If Banzo came, he would be ready, rain or no rain. And if Banzo let him rest, he would rest deeply, ready for whatever the next day brought. Either way, he felt no fear. Only a quiet resolve, as steady as the falling rain.

The night deepened, and Matajuro slept the light sleep of a warrior, one ear open to the world, yet mind at peace, floating on the edge of dreams where wooden swords and falling raindrops mixed and danced.

Tomorrow would come, and with it, likely, more blows. But he no longer resented them. They were the shape of his world, and within that shape, he was finding himself.

PART IV – EDGE WITHOUT EDGE

*The warrior whose spirit is sharp carries an edge
no steel can match.*

By the time winter arrived again on Mount Futara, Matajuro's transformation was unmistakable. In the dim predawn light, he could be seen moving through the clearing with a quiet assurance—feeding the fire, carrying water, his steps light, his senses open to every stirring of wind. The snow lay thick on the ground, muffling sound, but not a single crunch of Matajuro's footfalls escaped his own notice. He heard the gentle thump as clumps of snow slid from pine boughs, the distant caw of a crow echoing off icy cliffs, even the soft patter of a weasel's feet tunneling under the powdery drifts near the woodpile.

And just as surely, if Banzo were to approach, Matajuro would know it—snow or no snow, silence or no silence. In fact, Banzo had scarcely managed to land a solid blow on Matajuro in weeks. The older man's surprise attacks had become less frequent and more calculated, as if he were pushing the limits of Matajuro's heightened awareness to find any remaining cracks.

One overcast afternoon, Matajuro knelt in the snow to split kindling. He sensed Banzo watching from the shadow of the hut, though he did not glance up. He simply continued with measured movements —raising the hatchet, exhaling, and bringing it down in a precise stroke that split each small log cleanly in two. He set aside the pieces and lined up another. There was a profound stillness in him as he worked, like a pond without a ripple, yet within that stillness lay coiled potential, ready to spring at the faintest disturbance.

Banzo stepped forward, crunching deliberately on the frozen ground to announce his presence. Matajuro paused and looked up. The master stood a few paces away, wrapped in a heavy cloak, the wooden sword as ever in his hand. The sky above was white with impending snow, and the air between teacher and student billowed with each breath they exhaled.

Without a word, Banzo flicked his wrist. The bokken hurtled end over end through the air toward Matajuro—an unconventional throw aimed straight at his chest. Matajuro reacted instantly. He dropped the hatchet and pivoted on his knees. His right hand shot out and snatched the whirling wooden sword by its handle mere inches before it would have struck him. The force of the catch sent a shock through his arm, but he absorbed it, sliding back a half step in the snow to steady himself.

He now knelt holding the bokken in front of him, its tip quivering slightly from the momentum he had arrested. Matajuro's breath curled in the cold air. Banzo's eyebrows rose, and a broad grin spread beneath his graying beard.

For a moment, neither spoke. Matajuro himself seemed surprised by what he had done, though his body had acted without hesitation. He felt the solid weight of the wooden sword in his grasp, a sensation both familiar and strange after so long not wielding one. It was the first time in years he'd held a weapon other than a kitchen knife or an axe.

Banzo finally broke the silence with a chuckle.

"Since you've caught it, you may as well use it," he said, eyes glinting.

He strode forward and retrieved the hatchet from where Matajuro had dropped it. Weighing the small axe in his hand, Banzo adopted a loose stance. Matajuro rose slowly to his feet, bokken in hand, and bowed slightly in acknowledgment. Though his heart quickened at this sudden shift—standing armed before his master—he maintained outward calm.

Banzo attacked without warning, lunging through the snow with surprising speed and swinging the blunt hatchet in a horizontal arc. Matajuro barely had time to raise the bokken and intercept. Wood met wood with a sharp crack that echoed across the clearing. Matajuro felt the jarring impact in his arms but held firm. Without pause, Banzo pivoted and came in from the opposite side, using the hatchet's handle like a short staff. Matajuro blocked again, the sound ringing out. A flurry of blows followed—Banzo pressing forward with swift, compact strikes, testing Matajuro's newfound edge.

Despite the unconventional "weapon" Banzo wielded, Matajuro responded as if in a choreographed dance he had practiced for years. Except it was no choreography—his body simply understood what to do. Each time Banzo moved, Matajuro was already moving in tandem, his blocks flowing into evasions, evasions into ready positions. Snow kicked up around their feet and the chill air filled with the thuds and cracks of their improvised sparring.

At one point Banzo feinted high then aimed a low sweep at Matajuro's legs. Matajuro, reading the intent in the master's posture and eyes, leapt back just enough for the hatchet's wooden haft to whoosh past his knees. In the same motion, Matajuro countered —the first true counterattack he had ever attempted against Banzo. He stepped forward, bokken stopping just short of Banzo's side, a strike that would have hit the ribs had he carried it through.

Banzo froze, seeing the wooden sword's tip poised a hair's breadth from him. There was a flash of surprise in the master's face, followed by delight. He hopped back and threw his head up in laughter, raising a hand. "Enough!"

Matajuro instantly withdrew the bokken and bowed deeply, his breath coming fast in white puffs. He realized he had not only matched Banzo's attacks but had been able to seize an opening, albeit pulled short out of respect. The knowledge filled him with both joy and humility.

Banzo tossed the hatchet aside into a snowbank. His laughter subsided to a warm chuckle. "Where did you learn to duel like that, hmm?" he teased, eyes shining.

Matajuro lowered the bokken and allowed himself a grin. "From a very patient teacher," he replied.

Banzo shook his head, walking over. Matajuro offered the wooden sword back to him with both hands. The master accepted it, but instead of returning to the hut, he walked around Matajuro, examining him up and down as one might inspect a horse before purchase.

"It seems you can hardly be called a novice any longer," Banzo said thoughtfully. "Your father's son, indeed."

At that, Matajuro's chest swelled with pride. It was the first time Banzo had directly acknowledged how far he'd come. The compliment to his lineage—saying he was truly his father's son—nearly brought a mist of emotion to Matajuro's eyes. He took a slow breath, steadying himself.

Banzo nodded once as if concluding an inner assessment. Without further comment, he clapped Matajuro on the shoulder – the same shoulder he had struck with a bokken on that fateful morning to begin this trial. "Come," he said, steering him toward the hut. "The wind's picking up. There's warm tea inside."

Inside the hut, Matajuro poured hot tea into two cups with hands that felt strangely light. Banzo sat by the brazier, stretching his legs towards the coals for warmth. The master seemed relaxed, almost jovial— his mood always improved by a good bout. Matajuro handed him a cup and knelt nearby.

As they sipped the bitter green tea, Banzo glanced over at the wooden sword now resting against the wall. "How did it feel to hold a sword again after so long?" he asked.

Matajuro considered. He flexed his fingers, still tingling from the spar. "Different," he admitted. "It felt... natural, yet I did not feel reliant on it." He searched for the right words. "Before, when I practiced swordsmanship, I always focused on the sword – the weight, the swing, the edge. Today, I was barely conscious of the bokken in my hand. It was as if my body moved on its own, and the sword simply followed."

Banzo smiled faintly over the rim of his cup. "Good. If you had been thinking too much of it, you would have fumbled. The way of the sword is the way of no-thought. Only then can one truly be free in action."

Matajuro absorbed that silently. He found it to be true – during their sparring, his mind had been clear, without the clutter of deliberate thought. His actions arose from a deeper place.

The days that followed brought heavier snows. Banzo and Matajuro spent more time indoors, keeping the hearth fed and mending tools or garments. With the thick snow acting as a buffer, the ambushes naturally decreased; it was harder for even Banzo to move swiftly and silently outside, and inside the space was too small for full sparring without risking broken items or bones. But the training did not cease, it evolved.

Banzo began engaging Matajuro in simple reflex games. One evening, as they sat facing each other, Banzo produced two short wooden rods. He gave one to Matajuro and kept one himself. "Strike my hand," he said, placing his left hand palm-up between them.

Matajuro hesitated—Banzo's tasks were rarely so straightforward. But he obeyed, flicking the rod toward Banzo's open palm. Before the rod could land, Banzo's hand vanished, snatching away faster than a blink.

Banzo raised an eyebrow. He placed his hand out again. "Again."

They continued like this: Matajuro trying to tap or strike Banzo's hand, and Banzo evading with minimal movement. Matajuro increased his speed; Banzo matched it with faster withdrawals. The game honed Matajuro's precision and adaptability further. Soon, Banzo added complexity—sometimes he would withdraw and instantly attempt to tap Matajuro's hand instead, forcing Matajuro to parry or withdraw in turn. Back and forth they went, rods clicking in sudden bursts, their free hands feinting and darting. Some exchanges ended in stalemate, others with a light rap on the knuckles for whoever lagged.

These exercises trained Matajuro's reflexes to an even finer edge. The margin for error shrank to fractions of a heartbeat. Matajuro learned to act and respond without any conscious delay, trusting his eyes and muscles to work in unison as a single unit. It was a state of heightened awareness and emptiness combined — a mind without fear or thought, an edge without a sword.

Between such bouts, Banzo and Matajuro began to speak more freely than ever before. Sometimes Banzo would share a story of his younger days—an encounter with a noted duelist, or a narrow escape during wartime. The master never boasted; he spoke matter-of-factly, often highlighting how cleverness or calm had won the day over brute strength. Matajuro listened eagerly, gleaning wisdom from each anecdote. He noticed that Banzo's tales often carried subtle lessons: the importance of observing an opponent closely, the power of patience in waiting for the right moment, the way a warrior's presence alone could dissuade violence.

One cold clear morning, Banzo led Matajuro on a hike further up the mountain, beyond the familiar groves. The snow was crusted firm underfoot, and the sky was a piercing blue. They climbed until they reached a rocky outcrop from which the entire valley spread out below in quilted fields and distant villages. Banzo pointed to various landmarks, recalling times he had traveled through them or people he had known there. Matajuro realized this was the first time Banzo had taken him beyond the routine of work and training to simply spend time together as companions.

At the cliff's edge, the master and apprentice stood side by side, watching the cold winter sun sparkled off the snow. The wind was gentle but carried a deep silence with it. Banzo closed his eyes, tilting his face to the sun. Matajuro followed suit. They stood without speaking for a long while, breathing the crisp air. Matajuro's mind felt as clear as the cloudless sky. In that clarity, he felt an immense gratitude — for the mountain, for the trials, for the man beside him who had broken him down and built him anew.

Without opening his eyes, Matajuro spoke softly,

"Master, I feel I have changed so much. And yet, I have not drawn my sword in all these years. The steel I carried up this mountain lies still in its sheath." He touched the empty space at his side, where once his sword would have hung — nowadays he seldom wore it, as Banzo's rule held. "I almost fear that when I finally draw it, I won't know myself."

Banzo's eyes remained closed, but a small smile came to his lips. "When the time comes for you to draw that sword, you will find that nothing under heaven is beyond your grasp," he said quietly. "By not drawing it for so long, you have learned to wield a far greater weapon."

Matajuro turned to look at his teacher. Banzo opened his eyes and looked back, the lines of age on his face soft in the midday light. Matajuro felt he understood. The weapon Banzo spoke of was himself — his own body, mind, and spirit, honed to a cutting edge without ever unsheathing a blade.

They descended the mountain in companionable silence. Matajuro's heart was light, and each step down the snowy path felt like a step closer to some inevitable conclusion.

As winter yielded to a tender spring, the training entered what felt like its final phase. Banzo no longer launched surprise attacks at Matajuro — there was no need. If the master so much as twitched with intent, Matajuro's eyes flicked toward him and a subtle shift in his stance signaled readiness. Instead, Banzo began inviting Matajuro to practice with him in formal bouts. Sometimes they used bokken; other times, long staffs or even just bare hands. These sessions were not to pit them as enemies, but to refine technique and understanding, like two musicians improvising a duet.

During one such sparring session with staffs amid the blooming cherry trees, Banzo suddenly dropped his weapon mid-exchange and stepped back. Matajuro halted at once, lowering his staff in concern.

Banzo held up a hand, chest heaving slightly. "No more," he said, but he was smiling. A rain of pink petals swirled around them as a breeze shook the blossoms. "I cannot continue without taking this seriously," Banzo continued. "And if I take it seriously, one of us may get hurt."

Matajuro wasn't sure he understood. He bowed and waited.

Banzo tossed aside the staff and walked up to Matajuro. He placed a hand on Matajuro's shoulder with the familiarity of a proud father. "You have become quick, strong, and clear," he said. "I have taught you all I can through experience. There remains only one thing."

Matajuro felt his pulse quicken at the solemn tone in Banzo's voice. "What is that, Master?"

Banzo's dark eyes bore into Matajuro's, and for a moment, Matajuro glimpsed the immense depth in them — like gazing into a deep well reflecting the sky. "To take up your sword," Banzo said, "and know that whether it is in your hand or not, it is one with you."

Matajuro's mouth went dry. He understood what Banzo was implying: the training of years, the patience, the hardship, all were to culminate in him finally wielding a real blade again, but this time with the unity of mind and body he had attained. It was both a thrilling and daunting prospect.

Banzo stepped back and nodded toward the hut. "Tomorrow at first light, bring your sword to the clearing. The time has come for me to see the edge you carry — the edge that has no edge."

Matajuro bowed deeply, excitement and calm washing through him in alternating waves. "Yes, Master."

That evening, for the first time in a long while, Matajuro went to the chest where he kept his belongings and reverently unpacked his long-neglected katana. Its sheath was oiled but plain, showing a few scuffs of travel. Matajuro sat by lamplight and drew the blade partway to inspect it. The steel gleamed, mirror-bright along the cutting edge. He ran a thumb gently down the flat of the blade. To his relief, he found it well-preserved — he had done enough with periodic cleaning and oiling to keep rust at bay.

He did notice, however, that the sensation of holding it was different now. There was no eagerness to swing it about, no trembling of untested skill. It felt like greeting an old friend after many years, both familiar and yet different because he himself had changed so profoundly.

Matajuro closed his eyes, still holding the sword in his lap. He recalled how once he had fantasized about flashy techniques and famous duels, about proving himself with this very sword. Now all that seemed distant, almost trivial compared to what he had learned in silence and obscurity. The sword was no longer the goal; it was simply an extension of what he had become.

He slid the blade home and placed the katana on the stand next to Banzo's wooden bokken. For a moment he looked at them side by side — one deadly sharp, the other blunt; one untouched for years, the other worn from constant use. It struck him that in the morning, the difference between the two might not matter as much as he once thought. A blade is only as effective as the hand that wields it, and his hands had been tempered in a forge beyond any he had imagined.

That night Matajuro slept deeply and without dreams. There was no anxiety, only a steady anticipation for dawn. In the still hours, snowmelt dripped from the eaves, and a nightingale's song filtered from the forest — the first of the season, heralding spring and something new awakening.

The edge without edge was in him now, and tomorrow the world would see it.

PART V – SWORD THAT IS NO SWORD

The highest victory is won without unsheathing the sword.

Morning arrived quiet and golden. Matajuro stepped into the clearing with his sword at his side, the first time in years he had worn it openly. A light mist clung to the ground, swirling around his sandals as he walked. Over the eastern ridge, the sun was just peeking, bathing the sky in hues of amber and rose. The air was cool and still; droplets of dew on the grass caught the dawn light like scattered gems.

Banzo stood waiting near the old cherry tree at the edge of the clearing. He too wore a sword—a gleaming katana that Matajuro had never seen drawn. It must have been Banzo's own blade, kept hidden away all this time. The master's expression was serene, but his eyes were keen and alive with anticipation.

Matajuro approached and bowed deeply to his teacher. Banzo returned the bow with equal respect. For a moment, they remained in silence, two figures facing each other amid the drifting mist, generations apart yet bound by what they had shared on this mountainside.

Banzo spoke softly, almost reverently. "Draw your sword, Matajuro."

Matajuro grasped the hilt of his katana. The rays of the morning sun glinted on the polished sheath as he slowly pulled the blade free. The sound of steel sliding against wood rang out—a clear, bright note that hung in the crisp air. Matajuro held the sword in a two-handed grip, the stance coming to him as naturally as breathing. Yet it felt different now—grounded, unhurried. The sword was an extension of him, not an object he wielded but a part of his being.

Banzo nodded, satisfied by the form and presence Matajuro exuded. The master drew his own sword in a fluid motion. Matajuro glimpsed Banzo's blade;

it was simple in design, with a subtle wave in the temper line—a weapon clearly cared for and deadly sharp. Banzo fell into a stance, sword held low but ready.

For a few heartbeats they remained still. Matajuro could hear the soft rustle of a breeze stirring the treetops above, the distant call of a morning dove. His mind was clear, free of any thought of winning or losing, empty of fear or ambition. He simply was, as present as the sunlight on his blade.

Banzo moved first. In the blink of an eye, the master closed the distance, his katana flashing in a diagonal cut aimed at Matajuro's shoulder. Matajuro met it smoothly, steel ringing against steel. The force of their meeting sent a small shockwave through the mist at their feet and shook dewdrops from the cherry tree branches. Matajuro felt the power in Banzo's strike—it was far stronger and faster than the wooden sword blows he'd grown accustomed to, yet it did not rattle him. His arms absorbed the impact, his footing steady on the damp grass.

Without pause, Banzo pivoted and came in with a thrust toward Matajuro's midsection. Matajuro turned aside, letting the blade slip past his robe by a hair's breadth, and countered with a swift slash towards Banzo's forearm. Banzo retracted like water,

Matajuro's edge slicing only through a swirl of mist.

They parted, circled, and clashed again. The clearing filled with the sharp music of swords—an elegant, controlled fury. Banzo attacked high, low, from the left, from the right, testing every angle and tactic honed over decades. Matajuro answered each with the appropriate response, his movements economical and precise. The mist churned around them with every whirl and step, and the sunlight now streamed through the trees in golden shafts, illuminating the duel as if the day itself bore witness.

Matajuro found that unlike years ago when sparring with his father, he was not consciously analyzing Banzo's strikes or planning his own. There was no time for such thought, nor any need. His body moved of its own accord, guided by an intuitive understanding of rhythm and distance. He felt a deep connection to Banzo's intent—almost as if he knew what strike would come the instant before it was launched. It was not magic or mind-reading; it was the fruit of countless hours of facing the master's unpredictable assaults. Banzo's slight shifts of muscle, the flicker in his eyes, even the pattern of his breathing all spoke volumes to Matajuro's attuned senses.

The swords locked momentarily, edge to edge.

Banzo's face was inches away, his grin fierce and joyful. Matajuro matched it with a calm focus in his eyes. With a twist, Banzo disengaged and stepped back. They were both breathing harder now, a sheen of sweat on their brows despite the chill of the morning.

Banzo lowered his blade slightly. "Excellent," he murmured, just loud enough for Matajuro to hear, and there was unmistakable pride in his voice.

Matajuro swallowed, steadying his breath. But he remained in stance; the duel was not yet over. He could sense Banzo gathering himself for a final measure.

Suddenly, Banzo dashed forward in a flurry of motion. It was a sequence Matajuro had never seen: a feint, a real strike, another feint, flowing like a cascade of strikes one after the other—a technique likely reserved for only the most worthy opponents. Matajuro did not flinch. In the span of a heartbeat, he parried the first slash, evaded the second with a tilt of his torso, and answered the third by driving forward into Banzo's space, effectively jamming the attack before it could fully form.

This left Banzo momentarily off-balance—his sword arm extended awkwardly and his side exposed. Matajuro's training seized the moment. Seeing the opening, he thrust his blade forward, stopping it an inch from Banzo's undefended flank.

Both men froze in that posture. Matajuro's blade hovered just above the fabric of Banzo's kimono, close enough that Banzo could feel its cold kiss without it cutting skin. Banzo had his sword raised at Matajuro's shoulder, but likewise held back from completing the strike. If either had continued, the other would have been wounded at the same instant.

Silence descended, broken only by the sound of their breathing and a solitary drip of dew falling from a leaf. A beam of sunlight broke through the branches and illuminated them, two statues caught in perfect balance—each the mirror of the other's lethal reach, yet neither delivering the final blow.

A slow smile spread across Banzo's face. His eyes shone with exhilaration and deep satisfaction. "Enough," he said softly, the same word he had used the day before, but now it carried a tone of conclusion.

Matajuro nodded and stepped back, withdrawing his sword smoothly. Banzo did the same. They stood facing each other, swords lowered.

Banzo looked at Matajuro long and hard, then broke into warm laughter. It was full-throated and unrestrained, echoing through the clearing and startling a cluster of sparrows into flight. Matajuro, catching the infectious joy, found himself smiling widely, chest rising and falling as adrenaline coursed through him.

"Well done," Banzo said, sheathing his sword with a decisive snap. Matajuro slid his own blade back into its scabbard and bowed low, respect and gratitude flooding him.

Banzo placed a hand on Matajuro's shoulder. His voice, when he spoke, was thick with emotion beneath its calm. "Matajuro, you have learned all that I can teach you."

Matajuro's heart swelled at those words. He remained bowing, eyes stinging with tears he dared not shed. "Master," he replied, voice humble, "what I have achieved is only because of your wisdom and guidance."

Banzo shook his head gently. "I gave you only circumstances. You chose how to meet them. And now," he gestured to the sword at Matajuro's side, "you carry a sword that is no sword."

Matajuro rose and looked at Banzo questioningly. Banzo continued, "The true sword, Matajuro, is not the steel in your scabbard. It is the spirit and awareness you have cultivated. That is why I say it is a sword that is no sword—because it cannot be seen or touched, yet it cuts through any doubt, any fear, any opposition. With that, you have no need to prove your skill with needless violence. Your very presence will carry the weight of mastery."

Matajuro absorbed Banzo's words in reverent silence. He thought back to all the trials— the years of chores, the endless ambushes, the moments of despair and revelation. Every step had been part of this forging. He understood now that mastery was not merely the ability to win a duel; it was a state of being.

Banzo walked a few paces, picking up a fallen cherry blossom from the ground. He held the delicate pink petal between thumb and forefinger. "Come here, Matajuro."

Matajuro obeyed. Banzo suddenly tossed the petal into the air, toward Matajuro's face. Instinctively, Matajuro's hand flew to his sword hilt—but he did not draw. Instead, he simply watched as the petal drifted down, nearly brushing his cheek. In that split second, he had known he could slash the petal in two if he wished; the reflex was there. But he had nothing to prove by doing so. The petal landed gently at his feet, whole and unmarred.

Banzo nodded approvingly, a twinkle in his eye. "Your sword remains sheathed, even when it could be used. Remember that feeling," he said softly. "Restraint, too, is part of mastery."

Matajuro smiled and touched the hilt of his sword lightly. "I will, Master."

They lingered in the clearing as the morning mist evaporated around them. Banzo asked, "What will you do now, Matajuro? The world beyond awaits, and you have a life to live and perhaps people to return to."

Matajuro looked toward the distant plains visible beyond the slopes. There lay his past—his family name, his father waiting with unspoken disappointment. Matajuro straightened. "I will go to my father," he said. "Not to boast or challenge, but to honor him with the skills I have learned. He should know that his son did not abandon his teachings, but fulfilled them in an unexpected way."

Banzo gave a pleased nod. "A good answer. And after that?"

Matajuro thought of the countless possibilities—perhaps he would serve a lord as a sword instructor, or wander as a nameless ronin helping those in need, or even retire to a quiet life like Banzo's. None of those destinations fixed themselves in his mind yet. "After that," he answered slowly, "I will follow the path wherever it leads, carrying this 'sword of no sword' with me. I trust I will know what to do when the time comes."

Banzo chuckled. "Spoken like a true swordsman and a bit of a philosopher, too." He turned and began walking toward the hut. "Come. One last meal before you depart. Consider it a small celebration."

They went inside and shared breakfast—rice, pickled radish, and tea—laughing and reminiscing quietly about Matajuro's early blunders (Banzo gleefully recounted the time Matajuro had fallen into the stream, and Matajuro teased Banzo about the rare occasion he had managed to startle the master with a counterattack). There was warmth and melancholy in the air, as both knew this was their final morning as master and apprentice.

When the sun reached its zenith, Matajuro prepared to leave. He gathered his few belongings: a change of clothes, some dried provisions Banzo insisted he take, and most importantly, his sword. It felt neither heavy nor light at his side—it felt like part of him. Banzo walked him down the trail past the torii gate where they had first truly met years ago.

At the gate, Matajuro turned and bowed to Banzo one final time, kneeling fully to the ground in gratitude. "Master Banzo, I will never forget what you have given me," he said, voice steady but thick with feeling.

Banzo placed a hand on Matajuro's head briefly in a gesture of blessing, then bade him rise. The master's eyes were a bit shiny as well. "Go, Matajuro. And remember: the sword that matters is here," he tapped his chest, "and here," he tapped his temple. "Keep them sharp and clear. If ever you find yourself doubting, return to the mountain and visit this old man."

Matajuro nodded. "I will. Take care, Master."

With that, and a final, mutual bow of deep respect, Matajuro turned and set off down the mountain path he had climbed in desperation so long ago. This time, his step was sure and unhurried. The trees, now budding with new leaves, whispered in the gentle breeze as if saluting him. Banzo watched the tall figure of his student until it vanished around a bend, the afternoon light streaming through the forest in the direction he headed.

Matajuro felt no sadness as he left Banzo's home behind—only gratitude and a calm resolve. He realized he was not truly leaving his training, for it had become a part of him. The mountain, the wind, the silence, Banzo's laughter, even the sting of that wooden sword—all of it he carried in his heart like an invisible blade, honed to a fine edge. He was walking into the wider world, but he did so fully armed with skill, wisdom, and humility.

As he descended toward the foothills and beyond, Matajuro's hand rested lightly on the hilt of his katana. He was ready for whatever may come, yet he hoped that he would rarely have to draw the blade in earnest. For he understood now the paradox that Banzo had sought to teach: the purpose of mastering the sword was, ultimately, to transcend the need for it. Matajuro smiled to himself, remembering how impatient he once was. Those days felt like a lifetime ago.

The road ahead wound through villages, cities, and unknown adventures. But one thing was certain: Matajuro would walk it with the quiet confidence of a man who had grasped the essence of swordsmanship —a man who possessed a sword that is no sword, and thus could never be truly disarmed.

With the sun gently at his back and his shadow long before him, Matajuro Yagyu left the mountain, on his way to fulfill his destiny with grace and without fear.

EPILOGUE – BLADE THAT CASTS NO SHADOW

The finest blade leaves neither wound nor shadow.

Under the soft glow of a late afternoon sun, Lord Yagyu stood alone in his courtyard, much as he had on a stormy night years before. The scene was different now: where rain once pelted the ground, golden light now draped over stepping stones and raked gravel. The cherry tree that had been stripped bare in autumn now brimmed with spring blossoms, casting dappled shadows that swayed gently in the breeze. Yet, despite the warmth and beauty of the hour, Lord Yagyu's face was etched with a mixture of longing and regret.

He had grown older in Matajuro's absence. Threads of silver ran through his topknot, and fine lines marked the corners of his eyes. Each day at dusk, he came to this courtyard to practice his sword forms in solitude, though his movements had slowed slightly with time. And each day, as he sheathed his sword at practice's end, he wondered about his son — the son he had sent away in disappointment. He had heard rumors, whispers carried by travelers and letters: Matajuro training in the mountains, Matajuro serving a hermit swordsman. But no concrete news of his progress had reached him.

Lord Yagyu lowered a practice bokken he'd been holding and sighed, looking at the petals scattered on the ground. He remembered Matajuro as a hot-headed youth, swinging his sword with more enthusiasm than skill. Had he been too harsh that night in the rain? The question had gnawed at him lately. He closed his eyes, picturing that final image of his son disappearing into darkness, and felt a familiar pang of guilt beneath his stern exterior.

"Father."

The voice, calm and clear, rang out across the courtyard. Lord Yagyu's eyes snapped open. At the open gate stood Matajuro. He was clad in a simple traveler's kimono, dusty from the road. A sword hung at his side. Sunlight at his back cast his tall figure in gentle silhouette, but as he stepped forward, Lord Yagyu could see his face. It was Matajuro indeed — older, leaner, with a bearing both humble and assured. His eyes were clear and steady, his expression composed.

For a moment, Lord Yagyu wondered if he was facing a ghost or a vision conjured by his own remorse. But the quiet smile that touched Matajuro's lips was undeniably real.

Matajuro approached and respectfully went to his knees, bowing his head low until it nearly touched the ground. "Father, I have returned."

Lord Yagyu remained still, his heart thundering in his chest. There was so much he wanted to say — relief, apology, pride — but decades of samurai discipline held his emotions in check. He gently set aside the wooden practice sword and took a step toward his son.

"You kept your promise," was what he finally managed, his voice low. It was neither a question nor an accusation, but something in between — tinged with awe.

Matajuro raised himself and met his father's

gaze evenly. In that exchange, Lord Yagyu saw no resentment, no lingering shame — only respect and a peaceful confidence. It was a gaze of an equal, not a defiant youth.

"I did," Matajuro answered. "I sought out Master Banzo, as you advised. I have spent these years under his guidance."

Lord Yagyu nodded slowly, absorbing the presence of the man before him. Gone was the fumbling eagerness, the insecurity. Matajuro knelt with a poise that Lord Yagyu recognized in seasoned warriors — a centeredness that cannot be faked.

A breeze drifted through, stirring the cherry blossoms overhead. Lord Yagyu's voice softened. "And what have you learned, my son?"

Matajuro gently slid his hand to the hilt of his sword and drew it just a few inches — enough that the polished steel gleamed in the sunlight. Lord Yagyu instinctively tensed, his warrior reflexes preparing for a demonstration of skill. But Matajuro did not fully unsheathe the blade. He simply held it there, partially drawn, and then, with deliberate care, slid it back into the scabbard.

At first, Lord Yagyu was puzzled. He had expected perhaps a flourish of technique or an invitation to spar. "Is that all?" he asked quietly.

Matajuro stood smoothly and moved to the center of the courtyard, where once he had stood in the rain trembling with determination. He extended his arm and pointed with one finger to a stone lantern that sat by the walkway, about ten paces away. "Father, may I trouble you for a test?" he said.

Still wary, Lord Yagyu agreed with a nod. Matajuro picked up a single fallen cherry blossom from the ground. "Please place this blossom atop the lantern, if you will."

Though mystified, Lord Yagyu walked to the lantern and gently set the pink petal on its flat top. The petal lay unmoving in the still air.

Matajuro stepped back to his former position. He drew a deep breath, then, in a motion almost too fast to follow, he swept his sword from its sheath and resheathed it in one fluid arc. For an instant, Lord Yagyu thought he glimpsed the blade flash and heard a faint whisper of steel. Matajuro's sword was now back in its scabbard, and the courtyard was quiet.

Lord Yagyu glanced toward the lantern. The petal he'd placed there was gone. Confused, he approached, thinking it had simply blown off. But as he neared, he saw two halves of the pink blossom lying on the ground, neatly cut in two. His breath caught. Matajuro had sliced the petal — a target light as a feather — and returned his sword to rest so swiftly that Lord Yagyu had not even seen the cut.

Astonishment flickered across the older man's face. He turned to Matajuro, who remained standing calmly, eyes lowered in respect. Lord Yagyu could not deny the evidence before him, yet what impressed him even more was the restraint he sensed. The precision to cut a flower petal without disturbing the lantern or the air was immense, but the true feat was Matajuro's self-mastery: the strike had been executed without the slightest show of aggression or triumph.

In that moment, Lord Yagyu understood: Matajuro's sword was under perfect control — drawn or undrawn, it made no difference. This was a level of skill that transcended mere technique. It reminded him of legends he'd heard in his youth, of master swordsmen who could win duels in a single stroke or cow an opponent with just a glance. Matajuro had, indeed, become a master.

Pride and remorse warred briefly in Lord Yagyu's chest. He stepped forward, his eyes never leaving his son. When they were but a pace apart, he spoke, voice low and filled with emotion he no longer wished to hide. "Matajuro, rise."

Matajuro obeyed, straightening to his full height. Lord Yagyu noticed that Matajuro now stood perhaps a hair taller than himself, and it made him smile internally.

Slowly, Lord Yagyu reached for the hilt of his own sword. Matajuro watched, hands at his sides, his face serene. For a heartbeat, Lord Yagyu hesitated, then, with resolve, he drew — not his steel blade, but the wooden bokken he had set aside earlier. He tossed it to Matajuro, who caught it easily, surprise flickering in his eyes.

Lord Yagyu took a step back and assumed a ready stance with his sheathed katana still at his hip, his hand on the hilt. It was the same stance he had taken on the night of the storm. "Defend yourself," he said, but the words were softer than before, almost an invitation rather than a command.

Understanding dawned on Matajuro. He nodded, sliding one foot back, raising the wooden sword in a guard position.

For a moment, Lord Yagyu studied his son's form — textbook, yet relaxed. The courtyard seemed to hold its breath. Then, with a sharp exhale, Lord Yagyu moved, drawing and striking in a single fluid motion — the famed Yagyu lightning draw. It was a stroke that had felled many foes and one Matajuro had never been able to evade in his youth.

But Matajuro was not the youth from years ago.

In the space between heartbeats, he sidestepped and brought the bokken down with a gentle, precise tap on his father's forearm before the steel could complete its arc. The wooden blade touched Lord Yagyu's wrist and stopped there, firmly but without hurt. Lord Yagyu's sword froze an inch away from Matajuro's left sleeve, the strike completely nullified.

Both men were motionless for a second that stretched in the golden light. Matajuro swiftly withdrew the bokken and stepped back, lowering it in respect.

Lord Yagyu glanced at his arm where Matajuro had tapped him. It was a clear indication: *I could have broken your sword arm if I willed.* And Matajuro had done it with such economy and grace — intervening without malice, stopping without excess.

The old lord let out a long breath he hadn't realized he was holding. He sheathed his sword slowly and let his hand drop from the hilt. His stern features softened, and something wet glistened in his eyes. Not tears of sadness, but of pride.

He bowed to his son — a deep, respectful bow of one swordsman to another. Matajuro, startled, immediately returned the bow even lower.

When Lord Yagyu straightened, he stepped forward and put his hands on Matajuro's shoulders.

The last time he had done so was to push the boy out of his home. Now, he held him close. "You have done well, Matajuro," he said quietly, voice slightly trembling with restrained emotion. "You have brought honor to our name beyond my expectations."

Matajuro looked down, a humble smile on his face. "Thank you, Father." He carefully offered the wooden sword back to Lord Yagyu with both hands. The older man took it, but then set it aside on a bench.

"Tell me about your training," Lord Yagyu said after a moment, guiding Matajuro to walk with him under the blossoming cherry tree. Petals drifted around them like a gentle rain, yet neither the father's nor the son's shadow seemed to move — so in step were they.

As they strolled, Matajuro began to recount the tale in modest terms: how Banzo made him do chores for years, how impatient he had been at first, and how gradually he learned without realizing. Lord Yagyu listened in astonishment and growing admiration, occasionally shaking his head at Banzo's unconventional methods but also smiling, knowing such patience had indeed forged his son's greatness.

When Matajuro described the endless ambushes by the wooden sword, Lord Yagyu could not help but chuckle. "That sly old fox," he muttered affectionately of Banzo. "He always had a flair for surprises."

They spoke long into the evening, father and son, exchanging stories of training and philosophy. Servants quietly brought out lanterns and a simple meal which they ate right there in the garden. It was the warm reunion of not just parent and child, but of two warriors finding common ground at last.

As the moon rose high, Matajuro excused himself to retire for the night in his childhood quarters. Before he left the garden, Lord Yagyu called out to him softly.

"Matajuro."

"Yes, Father?"

Lord Yagyu regarded his son in the silver moonlight. Matajuro's silhouette was strong and upright. The father recalled the phrase that had circled his mind for months as he pondered Banzo's teachings: *the blade that casts no shadow.* He realized now what it meant.

"You have learned the innermost secret of our art — something even I had not mastered at your age," he said. "Your sword strikes true, yet leaves no trace of arrogance or cruelty. It casts no shadow on your soul, nor on those you protect."

Matajuro felt a warmth in his chest at his father's

words. He bowed. "I will strive to keep it so, Father."

Lord Yagyu inclined his head. In the gentle night, with petals falling and the lantern light flickering, he saw not the shadow of the once eager boy he had admonished, but the steady glow of a man who had forged himself in the fires of patience and perseverance.

As Matajuro departed for his chambers, Lord Yagyu remained in the garden a while longer. The events of the day replayed in his mind, and he found himself at peace. His son had returned not only as a master swordsman, but as a wise and calm soul. There was no resentment in Matajuro, no need for revenge or vindication — only filial respect and genuine humility. The elder samurai realized that, indeed, Matajuro's blade carried no shadow of ego.

A gentle wind sighed through the cherry blossoms, and Lord Yagyu closed his eyes, offering a silent prayer of thanks to Master Banzo in the distant mountains, and for Matajuro's safe return. Under the moon's gaze, he felt the weight of a legacy passing on, lighter and brighter than it had ever been.

In the days that followed, word quietly spread through the Yagyu clan and beyond that Matajuro had come back transformed. Those who witnessed him practice in the courtyard whispered that his sword was like lightning and that in his movements was a profound silence. They spoke of how he could stop an aggressor with a single, gentle strike, and how, despite his unmatched skill, he carried himself with the humility of one who sees no need to prove himself. It was said that Matajuro Yagyu's blade was so swift and refined that it cast no shadow — that one never saw the strike that felled a target, only the stillness after.

Matajuro himself paid little mind to rumors. He devoted himself to teaching the younger disciples of his family and caring for his aging father. In every lesson he passed on, he emphasized not speed or power, but clarity of mind and purity of intent. Many years later, his teachings would become foundational, and students would marvel at the philosophy of the sword that is no sword.

But in the quiet moments, when Matsuro stood alone in the garden beneath swaying branches, he often thought back to Master Banzo and the mountain hermitage. He would recall the sound of rain on the thatch roof, the sting of a wooden sword keeping him awake and aware under the stars, the feeling of chopping wood in summer heat, and the taste of miso shared in silence. These memories were like well-worn stones in the stream of his mind, their sharp edges smoothed to wisdom.

On one such evening, as Matajuro watched the sun set in hues of orange and purple, he drew his sword slowly and performed a single perfect cut through the empty air. The blade moved so fluidly it seemed not to disturb even a mote of dust. In that motion, Matajuro felt the presence of Banzo, of his father, of all the teachers and trials that had led him here. The sword glinted once in the twilight, then was still.

He sheathed his katana and observed the deepening shadows of dusk. There was no enemy to face, no audience to impress — only the profound peace earned through years of dedication. Matajuro smiled softly. His blade, indeed, cast no shadow in this world, for it lived in the core of light within his spirit.

He turned and stepped inside as night fell, leaving the garden empty and tranquil. The wind picked up slightly, rattling the branches and sending a flurry of petals dancing into the air where, moments before, Matajuro had stood. They swirled under the moonlight, then drifted gently to the ground, settling into stillness — as silent and untraceable as the passing of a true master.

www.ingramcontent.com/pod-product-compliance
Lightning Source LLC
Chambersburg PA
CBHW021930170626
46807CB00007B/3049